W9-BXA-720

0 00 30 0441815 2

For information address Disney Press, 114 Fifth Avenue, New York, New York, 10011-5690.

Printed in the United States of America

First Edition

10 9 8 7 6 5 4 3 2 1

Library of Congress Catalog Card number on file.

ISBN 978-1-4231-1455-0

Visit www.disneybooks.com

b18354725

Disney · PIXAR
THE WORLD OF
Cars

Meet the Cars

Disney
PRESS

NEW YORK

Lightning McQueen and Team Rust-eze

Lightning McQueen

Lightning McQueen is a hotshot rookie race car, poised to become the youngest car ever to win the Piston Cup Championship. McQueen is built for speed and has just two things on his mind: winning and the perks that come with it.

In his fast-paced life, he has little time for anything or anyone. But who needs friends when you've got a stadium full of fans?

VEHICLE TYPE: Handmade, One-of-a-Kind 2006 Race Car

Mack

Mack spends endless days and sleepless nights crisscrossing the country. For some, this life would quickly grow old. But not for Mack. He knows how important his role is. He drives for Lightning McQueen, the world's fastest race car. He's part of the team, and everyone knows there's no "I" in team, just like there's no "I" in Mack.

VEHICLE TYPE: Mack Semi-Hauler

Not Chuck

His name is not Chuck, not Chucky, not Chuckmeister, not Chaz, not Chet, not Charlie, and not Charles. He's a firm believer that a racer is only as good as his tires are fresh, so his motto is, "Change them early and change them often."

VEHICLE TYPE: 2003 Nemomatic Propane-Powered/Forklift

Dusty Rust-eze

Dusty and his brother, Rusty, like to help out their fellow rusty cars almost as much as they like telling jokes. That is why they invented Rust-eze Medicated Bumper Ointment. Whether it's some browning around the wheel well or a bumper that's completely falling off, Rusty and Dusty are there with a can of Rust-eze to fix it, or at least ease the burning, itching, and soreness that plague so many cars.

VEHICLE TYPE: 1967 Dodge A100 Van

Rusty Rust-eze

Rusty and his brother, Dusty, created a small empire out of their mother's garage in Boston. It's been over fifteen years, and their mother has watched their operation grow into a household name, with factories all over the country. Rusty and Dusty's mother says she couldn't be more proud of her two boys' accomplishments, but she hopes that their next big move will be out of her garage.

VEHICLE TYPE: 1963 Dodge Dart

The Cars of Radiator Springs and Ornament Valley

Sally

Sally grew tired of her life in the fast lane as a high-powered attorney in Los Angeles, so she made a new start in the small town of Radiator Springs. Charming, intelligent, and witty, she became the town attorney. She also became the car most dedicated to preserving the town's historical beauty. She even bought a motel and restored it to its original condition, and she has no plans of stopping there. She'd fix the town building by building if that's what it took.

VEHICLE TYPE: 2002 Porsche Carrera

Mater

Mater's a good ol' boy with a big heart, and he's the only tow truck in Radiator Springs. Mater runs Tow-Mater Towing and Salvage and manages the local impound lot. Though a little rusty, he has the quickest tow rope in Carburetor County and is always the first to lend a helping hand. Mater sees the bright side of any situation. He's the heart and soul of Radiator Springs. He doesn't have a mean bolt on his chassis.

VEHICLE TYPE: | Haulital Hook'em

Doc Hudson

Doc Hudson is a car of few words but many talents. He not only serves as the town judge, he's also Radiator Springs' resident doctor. Doc is respected and admired by the townsfolk for the way he looks out for their health and tends to their aches and pains. No one knows too much about Doc's life before he came to town. He keeps his private life private. But if you've got a bad spark plug or a rattle in your engine, his door is always open.

VEHICLE TYPE: | 1951 Hudson Hornet

Flo

Flo first arrived in Radiator Springs as a touring Motorama girl in the fifties. She was headed west with a group of models when her chaperone got fuel-pump problems just outside of town. Flo and the other show-car girls spent an unforgettable night in Radiator Springs. While she was there, Flo's paint got scratched. But when she went to Ramone for a paint job, he refused. It wasn't because he was too good to paint her, but because she was too good to be painted. When the girls left, Flo stayed. She and Ramone have been together ever since.

VEHICLE TYPE: 1956 Show Car

Ramone

A true artist isn't afraid to take chances, explore new ways to express himself, or push the limits of culture. Ramone believes that the automotive body can be a vehicle of expression. Every day gives him a chance to explore new paint jobs and to push the limitless boundaries of his art.

VEHICLE TYPE: 1959 Chevrolet Impala

Luigi

Luigi runs the local tire shop in Radiator Springs, Luigi's Casa Della Tires. If you're going to drive through this world, why not look good doing it? That's Luigi's motto. Cars may not get to choose their body type, but they all have a choice when it comes to the tires they wear. Luigi offers the finest selection of tires west of the Mississippi. Luigi's Casa Della Tires is known far and wide for impeccable service, competitive prices and, of course, its very stylish owner.

VEHICLE TYPE: 1959 Fiat 500

Guido

Like his boss, Luigi, Guido is a huge Ferrari racing fan. He dreams of being part of a real pit crew for a real race car. To better prepare himself, he practices tire changes at night on a wooden frame he built in his garage. One of these days, he hopes to set a new world record for the fastest pit stop of all time. But until that happens, he'll keep trying to learn new things. Currently, Guido is reading *Tire Changes for the Soul*, and *Four Tires, One Goal*.

VEHICLE TYPE: Tutto Forklift

Sheriff

There's a long history of law enforcement in Sheriff's family. His father was a traffic cop. So were his aunt, his uncle, his two cousins on his mother's side, and his little brother. Even his grandfather was a traffic cop in New York around the turn of the century. Sheriff always knew he, too, would be a cop. After all, how many other options did he have with a name like Sheriff?

VEHICLE TYPE: 1949 Mercury Police Cruiser

Red

Red may not be a fire truck of many words, but what he doesn't say, he shows through his generous actions. Whether it's putting out a tire fire or caring for the beautiful flowers of Radiator Springs, Red is there to support and protect his beloved town. Red takes negative comments about his town very personally. So if you have something bad to say about Radiator Springs, you'd better watch out. Because if there's one thing Red is not afraid of, it's his emotions.

VEHICLE TYPE: 1950s Torchy Truck Co. Fire Truck

Sarge

Sarge loves to tell stories about his daring fearlessness in the military. One time, one of his tank friends lost a track in the Battle of the Bulge and Sarge towed him to safety. For his bravery, Sarge received the Grille Badge of True Metal! This and medals like it are displayed front and center at Sarge's Surplus Hut, right next to Sarge's own brand of The Mother Road survival kit. He guarantees that if you break down, his kit will get you through the night—or the next world war. Even better, it all stows nicely in your trunk.

VEHICLE TYPE: 1942 WWII Willy's Army Jeep

Fillmore

Fillmore is Radiator Springs' resident hippie. A believer in individuality and all things natural, he brews his own organic fuel and preaches about its many benefits. Visitors can try Fillmore's special flavors in the tasting room behind his love-bead and tie-dye-covered geodesic dome. His many conspiracy theories and "naturally" unkempt yard drive his neighbor Sarge absolutely crazy.

VEHICLE TYPE: 1960 Volkswagen Bus

Lizzie

When Lizzie first rolled into Radiator Springs in 1927, it was love at first sight—love for the town itself and love for Stanley, the town founder. But she kept Stanley on the soft shoulder for months. Then one day, she realized that Stanley's vision for a new oasis in the desert had become her dream, too. From that day on, they became the heart and soul of the town—and a couple that was never apart.

VEHICLE TYPE: | **1923 Ford Model T 2-Door Sedan**

Stanley

The statue of Stanley marks the very spot where Radiator Springs was founded. As he was traveling west, searching for a place to settle and make his fortune, Stanley stumbled upon a natural spring coming up from the earth. He stopped to fill his radiator and never left. Soon afterward, Stanley met Lizzie, the love of his life. Together they founded the town of Radiator Springs, which soon became a legendary resting spot for travelers.

VEHICLE TYPE: | **McVaporloch Motor Co., Locomobile**

Bessie

Bessie is Radiator Springs' resident road-paving machine. Everyone agrees she's a low-maintenance gal, but more than one unsuspecting hitcher has learned her quirks the hard way. Doc likes to say laying asphalt with Bessie is more like dancing than paving. Fill her with kerosene, gravel, and tar, and she'll produce the most beautiful ribbon of blacktop you've ever laid rubber on. But you don't want to pull her too fast or get her steamed up. Bessie has two huge buckets of molten tar and she knows how to use them. Just ask Lightning McQueen!

VEHICLE TYPE: *Basic Service Equipment Road-Paving Machine*

Frank (The Combine)

Frank is a hard worker. He spends his days in the fields, harvesting, threshing, and clearing grain. Then it's off to oversee the tractors' work for the rest of the afternoon. By the end of his long day, Frank is ready to power down for the night and prepare for the early morning ahead. So if you're planning to wake Frank up, you'd better have a good reason, or a really good escape route.

VEHICLE TYPE: *XXL MetroActual Combine*

Tractor

Tractors are hard workers. They enjoy what they do, plowing through the fields on a nice day and then falling asleep in the moonlight. But every so often, they wake up to the sounds of snorting and giggling in the distance, and they find themselves lying on their backs staring up at the stars. But they don't mind. It's actually kind of nice to sleep lying down for a change.

VEHICLE TYPE: *Axel Chompers, 4-Cylinder, Diesel-Powered, Easily Frightened Transmission*

Dustin Mellows

Dustin Mellows was a delivery truck for Trophy Sparkplugs in the 1950s. The mild-mannered van had a monthly route that took him through Radiator Springs. On one of his regular stops in town, Dustin had a near head-on collision with one of the locals. It all worked out, though. The two cars fell in love and moved to the nearby suburb of Couperville, where they are now enjoying a relaxing retirement together.

VEHICLE TYPE: *Emerycraft/Delivery Truck*

Alarm Clock

When Sally redid her motel, she wanted every guest who stayed there to wake up with a smile. This original Novelty Clock Car from the 1960s really does the trick.

VEHICLE TYPE: *1960s Novelty Clock Car*

Timothy Timezone

Hot on the trail of suspected bank robbers, bounty hunter Timothy Timezone found himself in the sleepy town of Radiator Springs, where he interviewed the locals at Flo's for hours. Ultimately, it was a tip from Luigi that led him to an abandoned silver mine on the outskirts of Carburetor County.
There, he single-handedly apprehended the notorious Gasket Gang! It seems the Gasket Gang burned through a lot of tires on their high-speed getaways.

VEHICLE TYPE: Emerycraft/Zinger

Greta

Greta has decided to get a full-body makeover and a hot new flame job at Ramone's House of Body Art. Tonight she's going to see the renowned body shop quartet, The Rumbles. The baritone, Chet, is an old traffic-school teacher who she hasn't seen in years, so she has to look her best.

VEHICLE TYPE: *Bruchman/Salmon Super Sport*

Mildred Bylane

Mildred Bylane first passed through Radiator Springs in the 1940s as part of a publicity tour. When she accidentally swerved into a bed of flowers, she found herself rescued by none other than the town's shyest resident—Red. When Mildred's job called her overseas, she left Red a single flower to remember her by. To this day, he keeps her memory alive by caring for the descendants of that very flower.

VEHICLE TYPE: *1944 Hollismobile/Driftwood*

Valerie Veate

Valerie Veate was a traffic analyst on her way to Portland to start a new job, when she veered off at the Radiator Springs exit to find a place to fill up. Valerie was immediately charmed by the small town. So she offered her services to the City Council. Today she is the head of the City Expansion Committee. She gives advice about how to preserve Radiator Springs' unique historical character.

VEHICLE TYPE: 2002 Cotswell/Senator

Nick Stickers

Nick's secret passion has always been bumper stickers. Fearing the looks he might get from his friends and coworkers, Nick never actually wore any stickers. He just bought them and hid them in his trunk. Then one day, he stumbled upon Lizzie's memorabilia shop. Her bumper stickers were so hilarious that Nick decided it was time to let it all hang out. Now, Nick drives down the road covered bumper to bumper with stickers. He's never felt so free.

VEHICLE TYPE: Brawny Motor Co.

Edwin Kranks

Edwin was a creature of habit: regular oil checks, dinner for one at Flo's every night, and a new coat of tan paint every year. Then, a weekend with some old college buddies led to an unforgettable night. He got a shocking, metal flake, green paint job. To his horror, everyone in town couldn't stop staring at him. But to his surprise, the girls in town couldn't stop staring, either. Edwin's habits didn't change too much after that, though dinner at Flo's every night became dinner for two.

VEHICLE TYPE: *1944 Piedmont/Hauser*

Derek "Decals" Dobbs

Derek "Decals" Dobbs came to Radiator Springs to find work with his old pal Ramone, touching up paint jobs and giving much-needed facelifts. Derek not only paints cars, he also paints murals. He painted a beautiful mural on the side of one of the town shops, declaring Radiator Springs "A Happy Place."

VEHICLE TYPE: *Hollismobile/Rumbler*

Oliver Lightload

Oliver pretends to be a long-haul trucker, but the truth is he just likes the Top Down Truck Stop. You see, he's actually an online stockbroker and he lives less than a mile down the road. He likes to pop in at the truck stop once in a while to crack some jokes, take a nap, or just listen to stories from the truckers who go through on their way to someplace far-off and exotic.

VEHICLE TYPE: Luxoliner/Semi-Hauler

Ben Crankleshaft

Ben considers the open road his home, fellow truckers his family, and the Top Down Truck Stop his dining room. He has few close buddies but makes friends in every town he passes through. Once Ben has met somebody, he never forgets their name. He can recognize a familiar grille anywhere.

VEHICLE TYPE: Northernstar/Semi-Hauler

Gil

Industrial waste recycling might be a messy gig for some, but no load is too big or too toxic for Gil. But it's the jokes Gil tells at the truck stop that he enjoys recycling most of all. The other trucks politely nod and chuckle as Gil tells the same old one-liners time and time again.

VEHICLE TYPE: Peterbilt/Semi-Hauler

Jerry Recycled Batteries

Jerry's a pretty easygoing guy. Nothing makes him happier than running routes on the open road. There's no one to report to, no need to wash every day. It's the best! There's only one thing that can put him in a bad mood, and that's being mistaken for a Mack truck. After all, he's a Peterbilt and proud of it!

VEHICLE TYPE: Peterbilt/Semi-Hauler

Race Day: Racers, Staff, the Press & Fans

Strip "The King" Weathers #43

From his humble beginnings on the Piston Cup circuit to the glitzy sponsorship and media attention he has today, Strip Weathers (also known as The King), has seen it all. This seven-time Piston Cup champion is the winningest race car in all of Piston Cup history. He's loved every second of his racing career, but, truth be told, The King is ready for a slower pace. He's looking forward to more time with his queen, Mrs. The King.

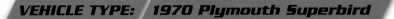

VEHICLE TYPE: | 1970 Plymouth Superbird

Chick Hicks #86

Chick Hicks is a racing veteran with a chip on his shoulder. He has cheated his way into more second-place finishes than any other car. He's been counting down the seasons to The King's retirement so that he can take over the coveted Dinoco sponsorship. He never expected such fierce competition from hotshot rookie race car Lightning McQueen.

VEHICLE TYPE: 1979 Shyster Cremlin

Chuck Armst

Ch
sligh
The
s

VEHICLE TYPE: Axxelo/Fission

Rusty Cornfuel
#4

Rusty Cornfuel grew up on a farm in Mississippi. He ran a racing circuit there with his buddies. Rusty won most of the races and almost made enough profit from the event to sponsor himself professionally. Luckily, a sponsor came along. Now Rusty can spend his own money on more important things, like flying his buddies from the farm to every race.

VEHICLE TYPE: Brawny Motor Co./Spark GT

"the Shockster"
#123

er
a.

Ruby "Easy" Oaks #51

Nicknamed "Easy" for his laid-back attitude and his slow, gravelly voice, Ruby Oaks's view of life mirrors his approach to racing. He likes to take it easy, gather his thoughts, get folks to let their guard down, and when they least expect it, take the lead.

VEHICLE TYPE: | Crown/Celesta

Ralph Carlow #117

Number 117, Ralph Carlow, is the little brother of famous Hollywood actor Jordon Carlow. The two brothers once had little respect for what the other did for a living, but when Jordon got a movie role playing a race car, he was forced by the studio to spend time shadowing his brother Ralph. After two long months of research, Jordon came away with a new respect for how hard racing really is. And after seeing his brother's performance in the film, Ralph gained a new respect for acting. Now Jordon never misses a race, and Ralph never misses a premiere.

VEHICLE TYPE: | Brawny Motor Co./Spark GT

Misti Motorkrass #73

Misti Motorkrass comes from a racing family, but not a racetrack family. Her brother Frank is a champion street racer. Her brother Zach holds the title as the fastest drag racer in three towns, and legend has it that her brother Dave has outrun five police cars in the past year alone. Misti's family is very excited about her career. Though she may not have the perfect track record, at least it's clean!

VEHICLE TYPE: Crown/Celesta

Lee Revkins #63

Lee practiced driving on the family farm. He recalls an old, rickety bridge over the river where he'd try to "thread the needle across that narrow bridge." Lee credits his nerves of steel to those daredevil runs. These days, Lee threads through Piston Cup traffic every Sunday, competing with some of the fastest cars in the world!

VEHICLE TYPE: Axxelo/Fission

Floyd Mulvihill
#70

Floyd Mulvihill originally trained as an automotive engineer. One day, he decided to put down his tools and pursue his lifelong passion to race. He competed in the Junior Piston Cup Pro Series with the likes of Sage VanDerSpin and graduated to the Piston Cup in 2005. He's affectionately known as "Smokey Floyd" because he enjoys laying long patches of burning rubber in front of adoring fans.

VEHICLE TYPE: Stodgey/Suaver EX

Murray Clutchburn #92

Murray Clutchburn's first taste of competition was as a member of the 1984 gold-winning Auto Games test track relay team. You might recognize him from specially marked boxes of Wheelies Shredded Brakes! After the Auto Games, he went straight into mainstream professional racing. Now he has a flourishing career in the Piston Cup series.

VEHICLE TYPE: Stodgey/Suaver EX

Johnny Blamer
#54

Johnny Blamer is simply one of those cars other racers love to crash into. He's been involved in more collisions than any other car in Piston Cup history, earning him the nickname, "Magnet Face." He's also known as the hardest working car on the circuit, though he hasn't finished a race in the ten years he's been competing. He holds the record at 545 starts and zero finishes.

VEHICLE TYPE: *Capitol Motors*

Kevin Racingtire
#35

With little natural athletic ability, knowledge of racing's rich history, or understanding of its complex rules, it's a wonder Kevin Racingtire has been able to last in the Piston Cup circuit for as long as he has. He says his success is because of his family, particularly his father-in-law, who is the owner of the large pharmaceutical company that just so happens to sponsor the team for which he races.

VEHICLE TYPE: *Capitol Motors*

Ryan Shields
#39

Ryan is not only the View Zeen Corrective Windshields driver, he's also a customer. Without View Zeen, the race is merely a blur of multicolored blobs moving at two hundred miles per hour. His windshield doesn't just help out on the track. It also has a special coating that helps cut down on glare while driving at night, not to mention it makes him look smarter.

VEHICLE TYPE: *Crown/Celesta*

Kevin Shiftright
#121

Kevin is the fourth in a long line of racers in the Shiftright family. His great grandfather Kurt raced on the old dirt tracks of the fifties. Kevin's grandpa Kraig won two Piston Cups in the late seventies and his dad Klint won three in the early nineties. Kevin tries not to let the pressure of his family history get to him when he's on the track or at the dinner table.

VEHICLE TYPE: *Axxelo/Fission*

Dirkson D'Agostino #34

Dirkson D'Agostino discovered his natural racing talent while working in a graphics department for a small racing outfit. Running errands between buildings, he'd dodge all kinds of obstacles at insane speeds. One day, Dirkson caught the eye of the racing shop's owner, who fired the young upstart for what he considered reckless driving in the workplace. Then he rehired him as one of his pro racers. He could tell Dirkson had a natural talent for the track.

VEHICLE TYPE: *Capitol Motors*

Slider Petrolski #74

Slider Petrolski's parents named him Slider after his uncle, famed dirt-track racer Slide Powers, who graced the gritty, makeshift tracks of the late forties. Slider wanted to be like his uncle. He started racing at an early age. He challenged postal trucks, taxis, delivery vans, and all varieties of unsuspecting pedestrian motorists. He even raced a police car, but only once.

VEHICLE TYPE: *Capitol Motors*

Sage VanDerSpin
#80

Youngest winner of the Junior Piston Cup Pro Series, Sage VanDerSpin entered the Piston Cup competition in 2004 already a highly decorated racer. His favorite trackside activity is dodgeball. Several other racers play with him as well, but it's the Pitties who are the toughest competition on the court, says VanDerSpin, because they're tiny and they have arms.

VEHICLE TYPE: Brawny Motor Co./Spark GT

Greg "Candyman"
#101

Greg loves his sponsorship, but there is one aspect he's not a fan of: the paint job. Gingerbread brown with candy-cane type would likely not have been the first choice of a professional graphic designer, but it was, however, the first choice of the owner's four-year-old niece. Greg also doesn't really enjoy judging the annual contest in which fans build a likeness of him out of real gingerbread and gumdrops.

VEHICLE TYPE: Capitol Motors

Darren Leadfoot #82

Darren Leadfoot is the LAST guy you want drafting you on the final turn. Known for suddenly speeding up at the end of the race, Darren is one car who won't let anything—or anyone—stand between him and the finish line!

VEHICLE TYPE: Axxelo/Fission

Haul Inngas #79

European racer Haul Inngas came to the United States in the early nineties. Because he won so many races on some of Europe's most challenging tracks, when he arrived in the U.S., lots of team owners wanted to sponsor him. However, one night Inngas accidentally drove on the wrong side of the road coming home from the bowling alley! Luckily, his ego was the only thing seriously damaged. He returned to win the Piston Cup championship later that year.

VEHICLE TYPE: Brawny Motor Co./Spark GT

Brush Curber #56

Brush Curber is considered to be one of the most consistent veteran Piston Cup contenders. Curber had numerous top-ten finishes in the 2006 season, but a string of midseason malfunctions sidetracked his run for the cup. With help from his Fiber Fuel sponsor and an overhauled diet, Brush changed his losing ways. He also thinks his recent success was helped by his loving wife of forty years, Katherine, and their fourteen children: Hal, Brush Jr., Penelope, Jake, Marty, Willard, Ingrid, Lucille, Scotty, Wendell, Aimee, Kassidy, Florence, and Truman.

VEHICLE TYPE: *Sherpa Motors/iota GT*

Winford Bradford Rutherford #64

An Ivy League school may seem like an unlikely place to get started in the racing world. Only a couple of years ago, Winford Bradford Rutherford was grille-deep in physics books, learning about momentum, velocity, and anything else that would give him an edge on the track. His doctor and lawyer friends at the country club thought he was crazy, but the studying paid off. Winford is now a highly respected Piston Cup racer. He uses his vast knowledge of physics to cheat the wind and outmaneuver his fellow racers, who affectionately call him, "The Professor."

VEHICLE TYPE: *Capitol Motors*

Luke Pettlework

Luke was The King's very first pit-crew member. The King's pits may have taken a lot longer with only one pitty, but they were done better. For years now, Luke has dinner at The King's house every Tuesday night, and their wives are in a bowling league together.

VEHICLE TYPE: *Nemomatic Propane-Powered/Forklift*

Gray

Gray always knew that because of his size he'd be hauling cargo across the country—gas, lumber, maybe even steel like his dad. But he never dreamed that his cargo would be seven-time Piston Cup champion, Strip "The King" Weathers.

VEHICLE TYPE: *Semi-Hauler*

Tex

Tex has been Dinoco's team owner and talent scout for more than twenty years. Sure, he's a smooth talker from the Lone Star State, but he's also a genuine guy with a big heart. He knows it takes more than flash and big talk to win—it takes loyalty, smarts, and a lot of hard work. And Tex ought to know; he started Dinoco with just one tiny oil well. Now he runs the largest oil empire in the world.

VEHICLE TYPE: *1975 Cadillac Coupe de Ville*

Dinoco Girls

Those nine blue-feathered beauties on deck at the Dinoco publicity tent are the "Dinocuties." They're the last dancers standing after a fierce competition in which the gals lived in a giant dorm and competed on television. On the final episode, Strip "The King" Weathers picked the winners.

VEHICLE TYPE: *Axxelo/Various Models*

Chick's Crew Chief

Chick's loyal crew chief has been the number one guy to the second place race car for over ten years, through the good, the bad, and the ugly. He longs for the day when Chick will win a Piston Cup so that he will no longer be the second-best crew chief on the racing circuit.

VEHICLE TYPE: 200 ½ Ton Truck 5.7 L V-8

Bruiser Bukowski

Bruiser Bukowski has been a part of Chick's pit crew for ten long years. Before that, they were in high school together, and before that they were in drama club together. Bruiser is Chick's number two fan, only because the number one spot was already taken by Chick himself.

VEHICLE TYPE: Shystermatic with a Mustache Hookup

Petrol Pulaski

Petrol Pulaski used to ride with the Eighth Street Carburetors until police vehicles picked him up after a downtown street brawl. Since being placed in a rehab program that eventually led him to his first assignment trackside, Petrol has become a role model for ex-gang forklifts everywhere.

VEHICLE TYPE: | *2003 Nemomatic Propane-Powered/Forklift*

Chief No Stall

A former National Guard rapid-deployment specialist, Chief No Stall takes no chances with his crew's safety! Known as the toughest crew chief on the circuit, he barks out orders so loudly that No Stall race car Todd Marcus could swear he can hear his directions on the track with or without a radio.

VEHICLE TYPE: | *Haulital/Lugnutter*

Stacy

Stacy works for Leakless Adult Drip Pans. She's a propane-powered forklift who likes living in the city and listening to country. She's no Guido, but she's pretty quick with a tire change!

VEHICLE TYPE: | 2003 Nemomatic/Forklift

Tow

As the official tow rig of the Piston Cup circuit, Tow has pulled his share of battered, weepy champions off the track. He's seen the top racers in their lowest moments, but he always respects their privacy.

VEHICLE TYPE: | Tow Truck; Houslital/Crew Cab

Dexter Hoover

As a youngster, Dex dreamed of being a real racer. But a four-cylinder compact pickup isn't exactly designed for the racetrack. Dex found a way to put himself in the middle of his favorite sport, though. He climbed the ranks from selling pennant flags in the stands to become top flagman on the circuit. His caution-flag pattern is a thing of beauty. If it weren't for Dex, the races would never start—*and* they'd never end.

VEHICLE TYPE: *Pabloloco/4-Cylinder Compact Pickup*

Tom

Tom is a Piston Cup race official, but that doesn't mean he's not a fun guy. Sure, rules and regulations are important to him, but he also enjoys a good joke or a fun prank now and then. He once switched the signs on entrance C-44 of the stadium with C-45 to temporarily confuse his fellow race officials. The prank worked like gangbusters and everyone had a good laugh . . . except Tom, who felt guilty and reported the incident to his superior.

VEHICLE TYPE: *Remirunabout/Orbit*

Charlie Checker

Charlie Checker is the Piston Cup's official pace car. Charlie wears his amber lights with pride. He's not what you'd call a horsepower champ, but he doesn't mind. After all, he's always in the lead and NOBODY passes him. That's exactly how he likes it.

VEHICLE TYPE: *Capitol Motors/2004 Econ, 6 YL 3.0 Liter*

Marlon "Clutches" McKay

When you're cornered by a mob of ferocious paparazzi, there's no one better to call than Marlon "Clutches" McKay. A twenty-year service veteran whose time was spent largely as an armored troop carrier, he traded in his bulletproof glass to pursue his dream of becoming a Motor Speedway of the South Security Team Leader. He loves nothing better than locking grilles with nosy camera sidecars and personally showing them the exit.

VEHICLE TYPE: *Capitol Motors*

Marco Axelbender

Never mess with Marco Axelbender. This former ATF pursuit vehicle received a presidential commendation when he blew out three tires during a high-speed pursuit, yet he still managed to catch the assailant on nothing but rims. Today he treads safer roads at the Los Angeles International Speedway, arresting scalpers and turning away the riffraff.

VEHICLE TYPE: Emerycraft/Inka

Brian: Park Motors

Brian thought it would be fun to sell antenna balls at the racetrack for a summer—the problem is, that summer was ten years ago. He had hoped to start his singing career in September, but one thing led to another and his part-time job became his career. But Brian enjoys the excitement of the racetrack, and sometimes when he's calling out "Get your antenna balls here!" over the roars of the crowds, he likes to imagine he's belting out a classic show tune over the cheers of his adoring fans.

VEHICLE TYPE: P-150 Courier/4-Liter V6

Darrell Cartrip

D.C. is a Southern gentleman and ex-Piston Cup champion, and he knows what it takes to win. He's in the booth with Bob Cutlass for every major cup event, calling the play-by-play and adding humor and personality to the commentary. But when the racing flag drops, he's all business. That is, until he shouts his signature, "Boogity, boogity, boogity! Let's go racing, boys!!"

VEHICLE TYPE: 1977 Monte Carlo

Bob Cutlass

Bob Cutlass is a world-renowned sports announcer. He's covered every sporting event from tractor pulls to monster truck rallies, including the last three Auto Games, but he's most famous for teaming up with former Piston Cup racer Darrell Cartrip to announce Piston Cup racing on the Racing Sports Network. Bob Cutlass is the voice of reason to Darrell's enthusiastic and colorful commentary.

VEHICLE TYPE: 1998 Saxon GTSC Grand Touring Sport Coupe GHi; 3-Liter Inline Six, 255 HP SAE @ 6,600 RPM

Kori Turbowitz

The smoky-voiced Kori Turbowitz started her career as a voice-mail operator. But her delivery of "You have . . . THREE new messages" was spoken with such flair and irreverence that the next thing she knew, she was the number one morning show host on the radio in the Bay Area as well as one of the top Piston Cup reporters on television.

VEHICLE TYPE: *2005 Luxomobile/Animatic*

Chuck Manifold

Chuck Manifold started out in the news business as Barry Pipenloo. But when he started covering the racing scene, he knew that he needed a name better suited for the tough nature of the circuit. As soon as he started reporting as Chuck Manifold, his career took off faster than a drag racer at a green light.

VEHICLE TYPE: *Capitol Motors*

Skip Ricter

Skip Ricter has been reporting about the racing scene for years. After doing volunteer radio broadcasts of race-day action in college, he got an internship at a local television station. He soon made his mark with the launch of his weekly race recap entitled *The Race Machine*, which can now be seen in twenty-three cities.

VEHICLE TYPE: | *Brawny Motor Co./Shindig SR*

Tim Rimmer

Integrity. That's the first rule for any decent member of the press. Tim Rimmer is not a decent member of the press, though. He's a tabloid photographer for a local supermarket rag. But even Tim wouldn't give Chick Hicks the satisfaction of having his photo taken while he celebrated his "stolen" Piston Cup win.

VEHICLE TYPE: | Axxelo

Chuck "Choke" Cables

Chuck Cables hails from the Midwest but somehow found himself in California covering the biggest race of the season! A live telecaster for twenty years with the Plainville Pavement Press, he recently made the jump to RSN (Racing Sports Network) and became one of the hottest not-so-mini-van cams on the news team!

VEHICLE TYPE: / **Pabloloco/Lugnutter**

Houser Boon

Houser Boon was the first photographer to coin the now-famous phrase "Show us the bolt!" He called it out last season at a press event, and Lightning McQueen actually turned right toward him and flashed his million-dollar lightning bolt. It was indeed a proud moment for Mr. Boon—if only he'd trademarked the phrase, he could have retired twenty years earlier.

VEHICLE TYPE: / **Crown/Celesta**

47

Mia and Tia

Mia and Tia haven't missed a race in over a year, but they'd be the first to tell you that they are not race fans but Lightning McQueen fans! Painted in his signature red and covered in McQueen stickers, the girls scream like crazy when their hero races. They scream like crazy when he poses for photos. And they scream like crazy all the way home just thinking about him.

VEHICLE TYPE: *1992 Mazda Miata*

Timothy TwoStroke

You will find no bigger McQueen fan than Timothy TwoStroke. He drove from New Jersey to California in just four days to see his favorite car in the legendary race! At the speed he was driving, Timothy shouldn't have been watching the race—he should have been in it.

VEHICLE TYPE: Emerycraft

Kit Revster

Sometimes Kit Revster can be found waxing and renting surfboards at the beach. More often he can be found closing shop early and hitting the waves. But not today. This morning Kit closed his surf shop for something truly special—the biggest race of the decade at the Los Angeles International Speedway.

VEHICLE TYPE: | **Hollismobile/Driftwood**

Polly Puddlejumper

A mild-mannered homemaker by day, Polly Puddlejumper has rooted for The King ever since he blew past her on the outskirts of Placerville one summer afternoon in 1989. No one knows about her secret crush—and she plans to keep it that way!

VEHICLE TYPE: | **Emerycraft**

Matthew "True Blue" McCrew

Matthew "True Blue" McCrew has been a fan of The King since the first time he came off the production line. In fact, everything in Matthew's house is painted King blue, including the lightbulbs. Because for Matthew, being a fan of The King isn't just reserved for race day, it's a way of life.

VEHICLE TYPE: Brawny Motor Co./Leeway GT

Fred

Fred truly is racing's number one fan. Some cars have better wax jobs or attached bumpers, but do they have the heart and dedication Fred has? Not a chance. Between Fred's racing blog, podcast, Web site, and daily call-ins to numerous radio shows, it's amazing he has time to get to any actual races.

VEHICLE TYPE: Stodgey/Suaver LT

Syd VanDerKamper

Each year, Syd VanDerKamper migrates cross-country to see his favorite Piston Cup races. Last year, on his way to the Los Angeles International Speedway, he swung through Kingman, Arizona, where he found plastic flamingos at a local garage sale! Now a permanent fixture on Syd's "front lawn," his plastic bird friends have earned him an honored spot atop fabled Redneck Hill!

VEHICLE TYPE: *1986 Cloud Chaser RV*

Albert Hinkey

Albert Hinkey is not only McQueen's biggest fan—known as "Buffet Master" among friends, Al can guzzle two gas stations worth of fuel in one sitting! Al is the biggest and best friend anyone could ever have.

VEHICLE TYPE: *1985 Boxomatic/Travel'bout 4XL*

R.M.

R.M. and Larry are the best of friends: these two can usually be found making trouble and takin' names on Redneck Hill. But despite their rowdy nature, they are true Southern gentlemen and dead serious when it comes to racing.

VEHICLE TYPE: 1980 Boxomatic/Coach/5.0 L V-8 Motor

Larry

Larry and R.M. know the stats on every team, which is useful since they always have a bet riding on who will be the next Piston Cup champion.

VEHICLE TYPE: 1980 Silverliner/Coach/5.1 L V-8 Motor

Johnny and Jamie

When Johnny and Jamie were young, they spent more time goofing off at the race than watching it. They've grown up a little since then. Now they know that it's silly to waste race time playing pranks and getting into trouble. That's why they now show up early to play pranks and get in trouble.

VEHICLE TYPE: Nemomatic/Menv

The Convoy Brothers

The Convoy brothers have never been apart. They do absolutely everything together. The brothers work together, they eat lunch together—they even have vacation sites next to each other.

To see the brothers, you'd think they were welded at the fenders, but they're not. . . . Not anymore, anyway, thanks to the miracle of modern engineering.

VEHICLE TYPE: Silverliner/Various Makes